First American Edition.
Copyright © 1998 Disney Enterprises, Inc.
All rights reserved under international copyright conventions.
Published in the United States by Grolier Books. Grolier Books is
a Division of Grolier Enterprises, Inc., Danbury, Connecticut.
Originally published in Denmark by Egmont Gruppen, Copenhagen.

ISBN: 0-7172-8541-3

Manufactured in the United States of America.
A B C D   1 2 3 4

DISNEY's Aladdin

AND THE
White Camel

GROLIER
B O O K S

Once upon a time in the far-off city of
Agrabah, there lived a poor boy named
Aladdin and his pet monkey, Abu. One
day, they met a magic carpet!

"Hey, Abu! This is no ordinary rug!"
Aladdin exclaimed.

The friendly flying carpet led Aladdin and
Abu to a magic lamp! Aladdin looked at the lamp.
"The rug is certainly special, but this lamp…"
Aladdin rubbed at some dust and…

…suddenly a big, blue genie appeared! Aladdin could use the Genie to wish for anything he wanted.

Aladdin wished
he could become
a prince.

Soon afterward he was able to marry
the love of his life, Princess Jasmine.

Using another wish, Aladdin freed the Genie, who flew off to see the world.

Aladdin settled comfortably into his new life with Princess Jasmine.

Then one day,
a colorful caravan
arrived full of
wedding gifts from
distant sultans.

There were many ordinary gifts: gold, jewels, precious pottery and plates. But one gift stood out from the rest.

"A white camel!" Aladdin exclaimed. "I've never seen one of those before!"

Neither had anyone else. The little white camel's legs buckled with fear. She felt shy under the stares of so many strangers.

Jasmine hurried to the frightened animal's side. The princess patted her gently, but the camel was still afraid.

Perhaps she sensed the evil thief Mohmar lurking nearby. Watching the little camel, Mohmar smiled wickedly. "That beast must be worth a fortune," he muttered to himself.

Jasmine named the little
camel Ivory and did all she
could to make her feel at home.

"Ivory still seems sad,"
Jasmine observed.

Aladdin wondered how to
make the pretty camel feel better.

He took up his flute and played a lively tune.

Suddenly, Ivory's ears pricked up and she danced!
The little camel was happy at last.

But that night Mohmar sneaked past the
sleeping guard at the palace stables and stole Ivory!

The next morning, Abu woke Aladdin.
"What's wrong?" Aladdin asked.
Aladdin followed the chattering monkey
to the stables.

There the guard
told Aladdin about
the stolen camel.

"Jasmine will be heartbroken!" Aladdin
exclaimed. "I must find Ivory!"
The Magic Carpet was glad to help.

Soon the three friends
found a trail of foot-
prints leading to a
lonely desert camp.

Mohmar came out of his tent and smiled.
"May I help you?" he asked slyly.

"We've lost our white camel. Have you
seen one?" Aladdin asked.

"Sure!" Mohmar said with a shifty grin. "Around here *all* the camels are white."

Mohmar showed Aladdin and Abu a whole herd of white camels! "How can this be?" Aladdin wondered. Would he ever find Ivory?

But while Aladdin stood with his mouth hanging open, Abu sneaked into Mohmar's tent. The clever monkey found a sack of flour. Mohmar had colored the other camels to hide his stolen prize.

Aladdin knew just how to foil Mohmar's plan—his flute! The prince played a lively tune. One of the little, white camels started to dance!

"Ivory!" Aladdin exclaimed.

But before Aladdin could claim his camel, Mohmar grabbed Abu's tail! "Leave now, without the white camel—or you'll never see your monkey friend again!" Mohmar threatened.

Aladdin couldn't let the evil thief harm Abu. So he promised to leave without Ivory and not come back.

Aladdin felt terrible about leaving Ivory with Mohmar. "I wish someone could help me," he sighed.

"Did someone say *wish*?" a booming voice asked.

Aladdin looked up and saw a familiar blue face.

"I'm tired of traveling," the Genie said. "How can I help?"

Aladdin explained his problem. "I promised
not to go back to rescue Ivory. So what can I
do to help her?"

"*You* can do nothing.
But *I* can have some
fun!" the Genie cried.
"I think Mohmar needs
to go for a camel ride."
    With that, the Genie
turned into a bright blue
camel and trotted off
toward the thief's camp.

The Genie raced
around the camp to get
Mohmar's attention.

The thief
exclaimed, "A
blue camel
that runs as
fast as the
wind! This
beast is worth
even more
than the white
one. I must
catch him!"

Suddenly, the blue camel knelt at Mohmar's
feet. "This must be my lucky day!" the thief
said, climbing onto the camel's back.

But Mohmar was in for the ride of his
life! The camel took off like a rocket!
Then the blue beast changed into a giant
snake, swooping through the desert sands.

Mohmar could barely hang on. "Whoa! Stop! Have mercy!" he cried.

But the blue monster only leaped faster! Soon, they reached the ocean.

"Oh, no! I can't swim!" Mohmar wailed.

The big, blue snake laughed
and dove into the sea. Mohmar
hung on for dear life!

When the thief was soaked to the skin, the snake changed into a dragon that flew high above the hot sands.

"Are you ready to give back the white camel you stole?" the dragon demanded.

The terrified thief quickly agreed to return Ivory to Aladdin.

The Genie returned to his big, blue self.
He told Mohmar, "Your punishment is to wash
the flour off your herd. And if I ever catch you
stealing again, I'll turn *you* into a camel!"

Mohmar was so
scared he promised
he would never steal
anything again.
"Maybe I can
get a job washing
camels," he thought.

Back at the palace, the Genie played a lively tune for Ivory and his other friends. Aladdin was glad to have his big, blue buddy back. Life was never ordinary with the Genie around.

Little Ivory was happy, too. The wonderful
white camel had found a new home at last.